JANETTA OTTER-BARRY BOOKS

A Stork in a Baobab Tree copyright © Frances Lincoln Limited 2011
Text copyright © Catherine House 2011
Illustrations copyright © Polly Alakija 2011

The right of Catherine House to be identified as the author of this work has been asserted
by her in accordance with the Copyright, Designs and Patents Act, 1988 (United Kingdom).

First published in Great Britain and in the USA in 2011 by
Frances Lincoln Children's Books, 4 Torriano Mews,
Torriano Avenue, London NW5 2RZ
www.franceslincoln.com

A catalogue record for this book is available from the British Library.

ISBN 978-1-84780-116-6

Illustrated with acrylic
Set in Golden Cockerel ITC and Baker LT

Printed in Dongguan, Guangdong, China by Toppan Leefung in July 2011

1 3 5 7 9 8 6 4 2

A Stork in a Baobab Tree

An African Twelve Days of Christmas

Catherine House

Illustrated by Polly Alakija

F

FRANCES LINCOLN
CHILDREN'S BOOKS

In southern Africa, Christmas comes during the rainy season. This is also the time when the stork arrives. Some storks fly all the way from Europe to Africa. The baobob tree can grow in hot and dry places because it stores water in its thick trunk. At Christmas time, its grey branches are covered in leaves and white flowers.

On the first day of Christmas

my true love gave to me a stork in a baobab tree.

On the second day of Christmas

my true love gave to me two thatched huts.

Traditional homes in Africa are made
from natural materials such as wood,
mud and grass. The walls are made of mud.
The roofs are made from bundles of grass
or reeds. Animals have their own shelters,
sometimes made from thorny bushes.
These are known as kraals or bomas.

On the third day of Christmas
my true love gave to me three woven baskets.

Not everyone in Africa celebrates Christmas
at the same time. In Ethiopia Christmas is
known as Genna, and it takes place on 7 January.
People go to church, where they light candles.
Afterwards, a special Christmas meal is prepared.
Sometimes beautifully woven baskets of
different colours are used to serve the food.

On the fourth day of Christmas
my true love gave to me
four market traders.

Gold, frankincense and myrrh
can be bought in African markets.
Gold is mined in many African countries.
Frankincense and myrrh come from trees
in eastern Africa. People buy frankincense
to burn when preparing coffee for visitors.
It makes a sweet-smelling smoke.

On the fifth day of Christmas
my true love gave to me
five bright khangas.

Many people in Africa like to celebrate
Christmas by buying new clothes.
Sometimes these are western-style clothes;
sometimes they are traditional clothes.
The khanga is a traditional cloth worn by
many women, which can be used in
different ways: a skirt, a shawl, headdress,
or even a baby sling.

On the sixth day of Christmas
my true love gave to me six women pounding.

Wherever Christmas is celebrated,
people often enjoy a special meal.
In Africa, maize is often eaten as
part of this meal. The maize is
pounded and then ground into flour.
In the past this was done by hand.
Today, where there is electricity,
women prefer to take their maize
to an electric grinding mill.
It saves a lot of time and effort!

On the seventh day of Christmas
my true love gave to me
seven children playing.

Children everywhere enjoy Christmas celebrations. There is always time for fun and games. In Africa, many children make their own toys such as clay figures, cloth dolls and push-along-toys made from wire.

On the eighth day of Christmas my true love

Nativity scenes are used at Christmas to remind people of the Christmas story. These small figures show Mary, Joseph, the baby Jesus, and all the people who came to visit Jesus in the stable.

gave to me eight wooden carvings.

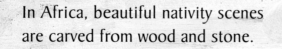

In Africa, beautiful nativity scenes
are carved from wood and stone.

On the ninth day of Christmas
my true love gave to me
nine grazing goats.

Flocks of goats are often seen in African villages. Goats are used for meat, milk and for their skins. Traditionally, it was the job of a child to look after the family goats. At the end of the day, the herder makes sure that every animal returns to the safety of the homestead.

On the tenth day of Christmas

Singing in Africa is joyful and lively,
with drummers beating the rhythm.
There are many different types of drums.
Most of them are made from wood.
An animal's skin is stretched across the top
and held tightly with wooden pegs.

my true love gave to me ten drummers drumming.

On the eleventh day of Christmas my true love

Dance is an important way of celebrating in Africa. There are dances for every occasion such as religious ceremonies, becoming an adult, and weddings. Sometimes a dance will tell a story or teach a lesson. Often people dance just to have fun!

gave to me eleven dancers dancing.

On the twelfth day of Christmas

Traditionally, grandparents in Africa tell stories around the evening fire to make people laugh, to remember history and to teach important lessons for life.

my true love gave to me twelve storytellers.

At Christmas, the story of the baby Jesus
is celebrated throughout the world.
In southern Africa this is when the
storks arrive and the flowers on the baobab
welcome the life-giving rain.

NOTE FROM THE AUTHOR

The idea for *A Stork in a Baobab Tree* came when I heard my own children singing African words to the traditional carol, *The Twelve Days of Christmas*, whilst living in Zimbabwe. As a family, we enjoyed Christmas celebrations in Sudan, Eritrea and Zimbabwe. They were special times when the values of friendship and sharing were particularly important. Polly's beautiful illustrations in our book capture this joy of celebrating Christmas together as part of a community, and the sense of excitement as these communities prepare for the special gift of a new-born baby. I hope you not only enjoy reading this book but also enjoy singing the words to the tune of the traditional carol.

The African countries portrayed in the book are:
Botswana – one stork
Zimbabwe – two huts
Ethiopia – three baskets
Tanzania – four market traders
Uganda – five khangas
Mali – six women
Niger – seven children
Nigeria – eight carvings
Kenya – nine goats
Ghana – ten drummers
Morocco – eleven dancers
South Africa – twelve storytellers